Taken from: Royal Commission on Environmental Pollution 'Turning The Tide': Addressing the Impact of Fisheries on the Marine Environment

'The light produced a thousand charming varieties, playing in the midst of the branches that were so vividly coloured. I seemed to see the membranous and cylindrical tubes tremble beneath the undulation of the waters. I was tempted to gather their fresh petals, ornamented with delicate tentacles, some just blown, the others budding, while a small fish, swimming swiftly, touched them slightly, like flights of birds'.

Jules Verne, 20,000 Leagues Under the Sea, 1870

Silent Agenda

by

Eleanor Pettigrew

My grateful thanks to:
Tony Osborne, in Bristol, who has helped me a lot.
Jessie, Sheila and Sally, in Yate
Elaine Lane, in Walsall Wood

A big thank you to Bob and Sarah for allowing the books to be sold through management and staff of **Buyology** Stores. All profits going to **Greenpeace**.

Silent Agenda --- I had the feeling this was going to be a salutary experience for all concerned, which set me on a path I had never taken before: to keep a diary: of detailed facts and happenings as they unfolded. My plan was to protect the spirit and character of the young men putting their lives at risk, should things go awry.

Chapter 1

It was Friday, the first weekend of the Easter holiday; James Potter frequently worked late, a few people tended to be around and he often did quite well.

The door pinged open and shut. A heavy bag, or such like, hit the floor with a thud. A customer had selected something too quickly and was walking toward him. People usually took their time. It could be half an hour before a decision to buy was made, or leave with nothing; with the bus stop right outside, sometimes they sheltered from the rain while waiting. He dipped wiped, dipped wiped the brush and laid it down on the easel and turned toward the slim counter, barrier between studio and gallery.

'Can I have this please.'

'Certainly sir,' Potter said, eyeing up the size and reaching for an appropriate heavy quality paper bag, taking the picture and placed it inside.

'How are you doing Potter?'

Potter exercised a policy of looking into the face of the customer as he took their money. That way he didn't go soft and let them have the item cheaper. Artists aren't necessarily good at evaluating their own work, especially if the customer looked like this one. He seemed to recognize the voice and searched the features through the hooded jacket shrouding the face, unable to shake the idea of camouflage from his mind:

'Prime minister what are you doing here?'

'Can we talk?'

'Of course.'

In one glance Potter had taken in every detail of the dishevelled sight before him. 'Take a seat sir,' he said lightly, and crossed the studio, slipped the catch on the lock with one hand and turned the open sign to closed with the other.

'How did you get here sir.' His respect, he felt, was vital at this moment.

'Car. She's visiting a friend, back in an hour.'

Potter, returned to his painting stool at the sales desk distancing himself from the PM. He still clutched the money and braced himself for whatever might be sufficiently crucial to induce a man of casual elegance into an intimidating scruffy anorak; to hide his identity, solely to enter his studio? There could be no other reason for the charade.

'Can I offer you a beer sir?'

'Thank you, Potter.'

'It'll save time if you take it straight.' He snapped

the caps off and passed one to his guest, 'No glasses anyway.'

'Cheers,' the PM raised his bottle. Potter also, before thrusting some of its contents down his throat.

'We need help Potter.' He blurted it out staccato, as though unable to contain the words any longer. 'We have a huge problem world-wide with over-fishing. We're caught up in an horrendous nightmare. Can't see any way round it. Fisheries are flouting the rules, you name it; the quota rules, the by-catch rules. The situation is totally out of hand.'

Potter found concentration difficult with the PM dressed as he was. He hadn't any idea how to react and heard himself say:

'Are there any options open to you Prime Minister?'

'What,' he said vaguely, 'Oh,' he said, seeming to recover, 'Reducing the size of nets, reducing size of catch, by-catch not permitted: It's too late for all of this: Between them they are creating devastation in the open seas. What sort of a world will we be leaving for our grandchildren Potter.'

Potter thought he was about to break down in the studio.

'I daresay they will cope Prime Minister,' he said soothingly.

'That isn't all, Potter: A Spanish Minister has been abducted; a French minister is missing; both are threatened with death if fishing is banned for the three months advocated. Yet I fear that's the least we can do, even those measures won't save the situation. We simply cannot allow ourselves to be held to ransom with conditions so dire. If only we'd had the courage of our convictions earlier.' His hand flew to his right temple, an action that appeared to have become a habit in the short time he'd been there.

'Do you have any ideas sir?' Potter was puzzled, what was he supposed to say? What could he say?

'We can't use the SAS, we'll be taking on the whole world, damned before we start.' He studied his hands while deliberating. So out of character, Potter had a distinct feeling the normally suave orator was embarrassed by what he was about to say, and thought it much easier to be a critic, than have to do the PM's job, with the weight of the job hanging round your neck.

'Potter do you recall the private army whose zealotry we had to curb a few years ago. Are they still intact?'

'Haven't a clue sir, but I daresay I can find out for you.'

'If you would Potter, soon as possible, there's sizeable funding set aside to deal with this matter, but, be discreet. Should things go wrong no person or country can be held accountable.'

'Quite so sir.'

The sound of a car horn startled the PM from his reverie.

Thrusting a card at Potter, 'My personal number,' he said, then bolted for the door. Potter followed and unlocked it. At this moment he didn't believe the PM capable of executing the simplest action with any measure of success.

He watched, temporarily transfixed in the twilight, as the car moved away.

The feeling of *de-ja vu* overwhelmed him, thoughts racing back to the closure of MI5 college at Hampstead and then back again to the Palladium murders. All contact with SAM, a private army, spread thinly across the world, had been lost and forgotten until now.

Lifting the two books the PM had tossed onto the counter, he locked the door to the studio and walked up the lane at the side of the building to the car.

Over dinner Jennifer was aware something had happened in the studio today. James was preoccupied, acting evasively, just like the old days when he'd clam-up and disappear, mentally, into his own world until the problem was solved. She steered clear; perhaps he'd had an altercation with a paintbrush, she mused, he'll just have to get on with it.

In the office-come-study, Potter picked up the sizeable 400 page colourful paperback and turned it over: The Royal Commission's Report on Environmental Pollution - Turning The Tide. He dropped it on the table and lifted the much briefer

Summary, deciding to read that instead. His mind slipped back the few hours to the actual happening: when the PM had tossed the A4 sized paper-backs onto the sales desk at the studio, 'Read that, if you want to work up some enthusiasm for the job. You can keep it. There's a whole lot in the backpack;' he'd pointed to a large grey bag, seams stretched by its contents, as it stood full bodied, by the chair where he'd dropped it.

'Oh right,' he'd said, eyeing it warily and thinking he wouldn't be carrying that, far.

'It's in your hands now Potter.'

'What is sir?'

'The state of the oceans for posterity,' he'd said.

'See what can be done, sir.' Potter had said, as though he was able to do anything about it, what a joke, the notion was laughable. The PM had to be taking the mickey. The whole bloody government can't sort it - all the governments of the world are helpless and now it's all down to him. He sat head in hands trying to get a grasp, an element of control, an understanding of what was expected of him. The Prime Minister couldn't go through any other channels. He'd used this donkey before, with success and no comebacks, so why would he go elsewhere? You're a victim of your own success you silly bugger, he ranted drunk with anxiety. He decided to sleep on it, concern himself tomorrow.

'Are you talking to yourself James?' Jennifer

called through the office door, not quite sure whether she should be feeling alarmed, or give the man the space he might be craving.

'No.' He replied, 'I've found myself a woman of charity, who will listen to the garbage I'm talking.'

'A woman of chastity? She won't do you any good.'

'Charity!' He said.

'That's alright then. Just turn the volume down, there's a love, I can't hear the tele.' She returned to the couch relieved that he'd sounded normal.

Potter was forced to smile at the absurdity of the situation. Jennifer always surprised him. Her practical nature in any eventuality had the calming effect required for keeping things low key and in perspective.

Chapter 2

Next morning in spite of a sleepless night, James Potter was dropped off at his studio. Jennifer needed the car for shopping, it was business as usual, the show must go on.

Potter, 5' 10" in stocking feet and weighing in at 14 stone give or take a pound, doesn't have to stand on ceremony any more. Although a D.I. with the metropolitan for a number of years, now admits to being a singularly happy artist with his own studio; fulfilling the odd order, and selling the occasional picture to keep food on the table. The family might well view his romantic idea of an artist's life differently. His son and daughter, both at university, if asked, may even complain of living on the breadline; he argues, studying 'social sciences' is the only way they'd know anything about the breadline. He mulled over the baggage of extraneous ideas that go with life as an artist. The excitement, nervousness, even the prospect of selling a piece of his very soul, for he treasured every moment spent at his eazel; frequently asking when he'd secured a sale, where the picture would be going and reckoned it worked out 50-50, for possessions sake or to enhance a wall.

What had he been working on before the visitation, he edged round the counter to the easel, then it came back to him. He didn't reach for a fine brush, to caress its slender lines as he was prone to do, but lodged himself on the edge of the painting stool his thoughts for some reason preoccupied with Jennifer. He smiled at the idiotic pictures entering his mind: She expected his jokes to be as original as his art. What's wrong with old jokes? Come to that, how much art is original? Then there's badminton. They play that to keep his weight under control, the biggest joke of all.

He looked round the studio his thoughts slipping away totally: A tall slender chap in uniform, normally in charge of the local police station, occasionally pops his head round the door, tongue hanging like a stray on the scrounge for a cup of something. He could see him there now, in his mind's eye, angular features barely discernable beneath uncontrollable blonde hair.

'Why ever don't you get that mop cut Barnes? You'll scare someone if you're not careful,' he'd said in good humour one day.

'Can't Patsy doesn't like it short,' he'd replied.

'Oo-oo! And she won't put her nurses outfit on for you?'

'Potter,' he remonstrated, 'you reduce everything to - - - If you insist, no she won't.'

'Ha - ha, ha - ha - ha - ha - ha, - ha - ha - ha - ha - - -'

They'd been bent over double and trying to hide from view of the window. Passers by had paused at the studio window, to see for themselves the cause of unrestrained laughter being thrust on the sedate community. Reluctant to interrupt, had moved on wearing a smile themselves.

Uncanny how they'd hit it off though; Barnes and he, colleagues on several cases, were different as chalk and cheese. Still with the force though, but can't be used on this occasion for that reason. He's going to be so disappointed. Potter moved over to look out of the window

Jones had been a much younger colleague, a wizard with computers, who pops in from time to time, has left the force, is building his own empire in civi-street. He could be useful in any enterprize without being compromised.

Lifting the brushes one by one he inspected each. His mind seeking relief from extraneous thoughts. Allowing him to focus on the immediate problem, which was what? 'Making contact with Bonnier.' He moved across the room, filled the kettle and tossed a teabag in a mug without casting a glance at the varying degrees of tanning working its way up the inside.

The PM believes the only way of bringing fisheries to their knees avoiding all-out war, would be through the secret army and Bonnier, who, with team and entourage, after a massive bout of food poisoning, had escaped from prison years ago and were never found.

In one movement, the brushes were returned to their sanctum and the mug lifted to his lips; his mind continued to wrestle.

Bonnier had changed his identity and appearance after being tracked down twice, so what would he do when tracked down a third time. Carrying the mug to the stool he perched uncomfortably, a positive attempt to put himself in Bonnier's shoes. He'd never met anyone like him: slight in physical stature, nothing ostentatious - a quiet charm, he had charisma - he was a people's man, fought for the greater good. Except for a period after his only daughter had been killed; beside himself with grief, beyond all reasoning, used others to reap revenge to ease his hurt. He had become judge, jury and executioner. Now the government needed him. Here was his chance, not to put the clock back can't ever do that, to be of service to the whole world. All nations had got it wrong but he and his army could put things to right: 'I think he'll do it!'

'Who what?' Jennifer asked, as she moved up and down the gears en route for home. Seated in the passenger seat, with a look of vacancy, Potter had jumped at the sound of her voice. He'd thought he was still in the studio, had stepped out of his body and had been mulling things over with, he didn't know who, himself he supposed, whoever it was, it was making sense of the problem.

Jennifer had completed the early morning shopping close to the studio and needed the car to get the food stocks home, unpacked and put away, before going to work. They shared the car, which James wouldn't normally need in his fairly mundane life of painting and visiting the local pub for refreshment and bon-homie. He was usually hard at it, painting 'landscapes', even copying 'old masters', 'graphics', (were liquid cash, all other forms of art pushed to one side until the commission was completed), when she called at the studio, but today he'd seemed vague, sitting looking into space; and in the car talking to himself as well as supplying the answers. She felt sure she should be concerned but there wasn't time, he'd have to sort it out himself or save it for later. Fred, the family labrador, was let out while she sorted the shopping and filled the cupboards, fridge and freezer. James more often than not took Fred to the studio, walking him in the lunch break, but not today. She glanced up at the clock, the hands moved faster every day; 'Fred,' she called. He rushed in trusting, expecting a treat. She dashed out in the same movement, locked the door and resumed the driving seat. Now on to work and James could have the car, and talk himself senseless, for the rest of the day.

Chapter 3

The last time James Potter had crossed Mark Bonnier's path was two and a half years ago at the newly refurbished theatre in Norton, when all 'the Royals' had been present, with security at its height due to expected sabotage; and there was the man himself, brazened as you like, seated in the front row of all places. Potter had known it was him, from his stance, the way he moved and slightness of stature, but with both appearance and identity changes he had remained free. He'd simply been out with friends, but anything was possible at that period in his life. Potter tried to imagine how he himself would react to the loss of his daughter. It didn't bear thinking about and he brushed the thoughts aside.

He had a hunch where to look for the man, any one of a dozen places; then sufficient lee-way would be needed to get the message across: that the visit was friendly, and could be of interest to Bonnier himself on two levels, without crossing his levels of security and the PM's boundaries of secrecy and diplomacy.

'Curse the man: Typical bloody civil-servants. Two things they can be relied on doing, is passing the buck and taking the credit.' Potter's tense features suddenly relaxed into a smile when remembering he was no longer an officer of the law but an artist, with a bank balance flagging for the sake of a little enrichment and Bonnier like himself, could possibly also need a little extra cash. We'd start with a level playing field. It's an angle anyway, he told himself, then concentrated on his driving.

Chapter 4

It was a strange set of circumstances which led to their meeting. The old haunts had seemed the only plausible path to follow and although no contact had been made at any of the addresses, the quiet indifference each resident had held, to the outside world in the past, was still apparent to Potter. He felt his presence hadn't gone unnoticed and knew instinctively that members of 'the team' still owned and resided, however tenuously, at each of the properties.

He returned to his studio, mid-way between Norton and the metropolis, mildly disappointed with the lack of success. Nevertheless the feelers were out, now all he could do was wait and hope for a response, if nothing transpired try something different tomorrow. His own need being as great as any of theirs.

Parking the car in the space behind the shop, he

walked down the lane at the side of the building and round to the front, stopping momentarily. A solitary man stood, hands in pockets, looking in his shop window. What a prize, if he was not mistaken, it was the very man whose stamping ground he'd just been scenting to lure him to the surface.

'Good to see you,' Potter greeted him with genuine pleasure, 'Come in,' he invited, unlocking the door; and the man he had known for a number of years, as Bonnier, followed him in. An arrogant underlying, you can't find me but I can find you in an instant, attitude was apparent, regardless, it had saved Potter a lot of time and effort. He was ultimately grateful, the man could afford to display arrogance, the government were doing the begging this time.

He declined the offer of a drink.

'Take a seat,' Potter waved him to the only chair, turned the seat he used for painting and parked himself on it; when settled, not wishing to rush things, then embarked upon the idea the Prime Minister had put to him the day before.

'How quickly we change sides when it suits us,' Bonnier said, with a bit of an edge, lips curving to part - smile, 'however, I will give it some thought and let you know tomorrow.'

'Principles aside Bonnier, I don't mind telling you I could do with the extra cash, I don't know about you,' Potter said, fully aware he was leaving himself open to judgement and ridicule. This was a proud man he was dealing with. If making a buffoon of himself encouraged success, then that is what he would do.

'There is that to be considered also; but would we ever have enough Potter?'

'Quite true. Oh incidentally, the PM left these books for you,' he toed the taut haversack, leaning benignly against the wall. Bonnier's eyebrows narrowed. 'Background information on the fishing industry, state of the oceans; each countries ownership of vessels; subsidiary industries; etcetera. There's a lot of them and they are heavy.' Potter explained.

'Interesting, I'll take a look later. Now I shall get my car and call back for them in ten minutes.'

Potter carried the bag, bulging with books, to the back seat of Bonnier's car and waited with reverence while it moved away.

Chapter 5

'Jones?'

'Speaking.'

'Potter here Jones how are you?'

'Great chief, but you didn't call to ask after my health, I know.'

'Well no. It's more a question of, are you on overload or d'you fancy something different?'

'I've left the force chief, thought I'd told you.'

'You did, that's the reason I'm calling you, although there's nothing certain as yet, but there could be. If the people decide on a course of action, I assure you, you will not want to miss this Jones, and there'll be a bit of spondulix for the taking. What d'you say?'

'You've bought me. When and for how long?'

'Should have a decision in the next few days.'

'Intriguing, what's involved.'

'Can't say, but you'll need to take a couple of weeks, pending commitment.'

'See what I can do. Ring you back.'

Potter replaced the receiver and sat mulling over how Jones, the youngest colleague from the force, would be reacting to the call. He would bank on Jones, in his enthusiasm, getting cover for his position at work, for possibly the next three weeks, in the first ten minutes after putting the phone down. Then he'll be out buying newspapers to get the assignment sussed. He could see him trying to work out what would be of sufficient importance for his old chief to abandon paints and spirit, then drag in the new boy from his growing empire. The vision hung before Potter's eyes. The force lost a good man when Jones left and he still in his twenties. But Julie, oh my God, he'd totally forgotten Julie; only best-man at their wedding and he'd forgotten Jones was married; will she let him go? He and Barnes and their wives had spent many pleasant evenings with the Jones' and he'd forgotten Julie existed. He could only put it down to single minded current stress.

Chapter 6

With the bulky haversack hustled onto the back seat, Mark Bonnier drove the few miles home; warm air rushing through the car's open windows caressed his skin with the tenderness of a loving touch. He and Wendy would sit in their tiny garden as though visitors, he thought, amidst birds bees butterflies and all the creatures we never see but have lived their entire lives in the miniscule world. He recalled having prowled around out there a couple of sunny days, threatening to enter the summer house slightly larger than a tool shed, to disrobe the deckchairs of their winter protection. A North wind had seen any rash thoughts off. He hauled the bag bodily, from the back seat, through the front gate, barely visible between the rich green hedges of yew, and round the side of the single story cottage to the corner garden, then returned and entered by the front door.

'Wendy darling, are you busy?' he called,

walking directly to the bedroom and French doors which opened onto the garden.

'Mark?' she called.

'In the garden dear, I need help with this stack of books.'

'Where are they going dear?'

'Not haulage darling, reading. I need to make a quick evaluation. I value your opinion, come and help me please.'

They spent the remainder of the day and the whole of the next day scanning and filtering the mass of information which the Prime Minister had left in the haversack for him to read. It had been gathered by The Royal Commission at the behest of the Queen, and paid for by the British government, 'You and me, in fact' he'd said, 'and no one taking a blind bit of notice of what it says. Sounds to me like business as usual in the political corridors of the world. It will sort its own salvation. Leave it to nature; in spite of man's desecration, nature will sort itself out. Damned typical.' Bonnier, nose deep in a section of 'the summary', had been muttering to himself.

His wife absorbed in reading looked up, 'What did you say dear?'

'Just being my usual cynical self dear.'

Bonnier found himself surprised, firstly, by the size of fishing fleets attributed to each country as well as the sum of the whole; although each vessel is allotted a quota, each has to have sufficient catch to offset initial outlay, running costs and profit margins.

And secondly, something his wife had pointed out: the continual thoughtless damage and destruction to sea-bed habitat ensuring eventually that all species would be on the road to extinction. Well all those that hadn't already disappeared.

'It's a noble task to undertake dear but I do think it too big a project. It's a question of self preservation Mark. You'll be hounded out of the country if anything goes wrong.'

'You know media opinion doesn't bother me my dear, but I would be happier if an angle presented itself - perhaps we need to view the task in microcosm and multiply the outcome.'

'Take one ship?'

'Yes that's the general idea. However I shall be guided by your advice my dear and turn it down. It can't be that difficult to find someone younger.'

'Quite right,' she said, nodding approval.

Chapter 7

Next day, unable to apply himself to any task, Potter hung about the studio in case Bonnier should turn up. He didn't make contact as promised, which wasn't surprising, there was a lot of reading involved: to get a feel of the subject and to conjure up some way of solving the issue.

Although guilty of many things in the past, he considered Bonnier to be a just, sincere man most of the time, and if, and when convinced about something, would follow it through.

Two days later Potter saw him arrive but couldn't tell from his facial expression what the outcome would be. It always carried a likeable yet immoveable mask; there was no knowing. He waived the offer of coffee or tea and sat once again on the chair in the studio, solemn countenanced. Potter silently reflected, it's an odd setting for the serious discussion about to take place.

'This is a huge task, Potter. I've given the PM's proposal a lot of thought but have serious misgivings. This assignment is much too high profile, affecting the lives of a huge number of people, for a part-time army to execute. It's okay for the Prime Minister to off-load his current problems - these are young lads who have to live with the after-effects - in a harsh world. I'm not sure it's a good thing to be doing - why should we put the men through this? I want to be convinced. Tell me. Give me your opinion Potter.' There had been no standing on ceremony, he'd plunged straight in, taking Potter's breath away.

'You know Bonnier, with respect,' said Potter, deliberating for a second, 'I don't see this agenda as a people thing - well only in so far as they will, or we all will eventually, in our shameful ignorance - deplete the oceans, regardless of rhyme or reason, of its entire stock of living creatures. I see what you will be doing, more as some kind of rescue programme for nature, and saving the people from themselves in spite of themselves. Have you worked your way through the books?' He thought the change of direction seemed the right thing to do at this time.

'Yes,' he nodded, 'I have to agree, it makes grim reading.'

The silence, which followed, was deafening. Potter froze. His mouth felt dry, the lump in his throat caused him to swallow hard, it sounded like a suction pump. But he knew the first to move would lose the argument for the cause and it was not going to be him.

After what seemed like an age, Bonnier broke the silence:

'I'll give it further thought and see what reaction I get from the team and SAM's officers. It might be my planning initially, nevertheless, ultimately, it will be their decision whether or not to see it through, they are the experts in the field. Then, and only then, with their agreement, would we bring the lads in for the intensive training needed.'

'I believe,' said Potter, growing stronger with the other man's relenting, measuring his words with care, 'in the event of you accepting this assignment, you will have access to a huge amount of untraceable funding.' Potter had relaxed the leash on the only credit-worthy plus, for the enormous task to be performed, hoping to effect a 'yes' decision. He noted that Bonnier looked relaxed although his face was impassive.

'Speaking frankly Bonnier, I thought the men might enjoy, even want to do their bit to put the world to rights, and with a huge cache available for the taking, they'll be helping SAM as well. Of course as you rightly say, there is the price tag. It has to be stealth all the way. There can be no come-backs. No country can be identified as being responsible, least of all the perpetrators. If things go wrong - - - . Well you know all about that.'

Whew, that was a bit of luck, Potter thought, two ace cards, not one! But which would Bonnier value most, he pondered: the honour of knowing what they had done, or the pot of gold, without which it wouldn't be possible. The two were inseparable; it was a silly thought.

Chapter 8

At Outer London Base Bonnier's meeting with senior officials of SAM, a secret part-time army spread thinly across the world, whose ideology, excitement and adventure, attracted many young men and women from all walks of life, had begun in the board-room. A huge monitor, hanging from the ceiling at one end, segmented into what seemed like a thousand different pictures; each representing a unit of SAM in another country.

Mark Bonnier at the top of the board-room table heads the meeting.

'Ladies and Gentlemen.

We have a situation here where the oceans are being flagrantly over-fished. Politicians abducted and threatened with death, to prevent closure laws being drawn-up between all countries and put into practise. Isn't that sad for the politicians, but I musn't be flippant. It is a positive tragedy for marine life.

The Royal Commission, with no axe to grind, from their totally impartial stance, have written a 400 page report addressing the issue from every angle; it doesn't make good reading. It's in everyone's interest to have a healthy fishing industry; but many problems have to be addressed, for example: The total extinction of hundreds of marine species, many of them familiar names, simply because they are marine creatures caught in nets from which they cannot escape; and are probably suffocated before they are hauled out of the water. Money is thrown at technology to catch the fish, in a very short-sighted fashion, without regard to the wastage, which could be as much as double the permitted catch. It sickens me to talk of it.

Please take a summary from the table, there's piles of them, get a feel of the issues at stake here. If we can cause delays to the industry, sufficient to allow time for common sense to click-in, then we shall be doing the world a favour. Although I'm sure the Fisheries and related industries won't see it that way. I fear it's a case of eyes which cannot see; ears which will not listen.

With this in mind, I have pursued every avenue possible, which might have a bearing on the outcome, looking for a workable proposition, to no avail.

The only solution to the problem I do see, which I think will work, is sabotage.

However, the problem is international: therefore the sabotage has to be collective, spontaneous, and across the globe. Attacking not only the ships at sea, but also ships in the harbour and dry dock, as well as all subsidiary industries.

For example: production of nets, sonar technology and other technical equipment; whose factories will no doubt be found in far-flung places, where costs of production are low. We have to track down every single manufacturer and supplier; dislocate all machinery for making nets and confiscate existing stocks. Similarly, for makers of sonar equipment and harpoon guns.

It won't work in dibs and dabs a little bit here a bit there. We have one attempt, one chance, which has to be synchronized and final.

Put the lot out of action.

Give nature a chance to recover.

At this point ladies and gentlemen, I'm sorry no questions there isn't time, you have to accept my opinion on this matter and make a decision.

Who is for?'

He scrutinized the faces round the table,

'And who against?

Now internationally - if you are with me, press your button

I need your votes. Who is for the Agenda: switch on your lights.'

The small light at each place round the

boardroom table, representing different countries, glowed like a string of very white pearls. His glance taking in every single one.

Bonnier paused, momentarily overcome by their show of complete trust and solidarity.

'Thank you members of SAM we are totally committed. I shall now take the first step by calling in all volunteer recruits.'

Members at the table watched, as he moved over to the wall and pulled a lever down; this activated a slightly larger than pin-head light in the entrance of every recruit's home, living quarters or bedsits; members are seldom called this way but when they are they move fast, it requiring urgency. When the warning light in the home is extinguished, it lights the individuals number on a huge board running the full length of the boardroom wall, saying each has received the message. This contact system is installed in all countries of the world, and their officers would be calling in recruits in the same way.

The members present studied the board with interest as the numbers lit up in a trickle.

'The lads will be here soon; we must adopt our emergency posts. Let the wheels of our organization start turning.

I shall adjourn to draw-up the blue-print, we meet here after dinner at 20,00 hours.'

Chapter 9

'Do you ever wish you were back in the force Chief?'

'Do you Jones?'

'Sometimes, not often though.'

'I can't say I've ever thought about returning,' Potter said, 'money gets tight, with the kids at university draining the resources. The family are sometimes fretful because we live on a shoe-string, but I love it. Something will usually turn-up to save the day. Jenny is working so she has her own income.'

'It's really good to see you chief. D'you ever see the lad, Bob Staines?'

'You mean the young lad who was very nearly sacrificed but for you taking his place on the plinth? Yes, he's a man now, well almost. I do the graphics for his books, what's more they're selling, how's that for success?'

'What about my old boss?'

'Barnes? Beat him and Patsy at badminton frequently. Couldn't get him involved in this business though, so had to steer clear. He'll be smelling a rat soon and being left out will peeve him, but nothing I can do about it.'

'He'll take it hard,' Jones said.

'How about you, Jones? Quite the entrepreneur these days, so I hear.'

Like being my own boss, that's what its down to, and although a country boy at heart, I love living in the city. You know the computer was my strength even in the force,

'Yes Jones I remember it well.'

'Did you hear chief? Mum told me the old boys, the brothers, were released from prison, through ill health, and are back running the movie club office, by all accounts it's doing well.'

'They've been forgiven and taken back into the fold then,' Potter said.

'Yes.' He thought for a moment, 'Funny we never got to the bottom of the brothers did we?'

'Unfortunately,' Potter replied, 'they were easily manipulated by their friends, but it's water under the bridge now.

Chapter 10

Potter, wishing to be as far removed from the impending case as the PM, travelled to Paddington by Inter-city. It would have been easy to lift a land-phone at this stage identifying himself, saying what he had to say, but he knew all calls to Downing Street were monitored, which could present problems later for himself and the PM. He set out across the city. Left the underground and entered a public call-box dialling the number he had been given by the PM, what had seemed a lifetime ago, but had only been a matter of days earlier.

Collar up, cap down, with most of his face concealed, he swaggered along Downing Street trying not to look shifty; yet the very nature of his appearance said exactly that and he knew it. There was no security on the door, the PM had seen to that, he wondered how he'd managed it, hadn't intended giving his name anyway. Ignoring official bells he rapped lightly with his knuckles, the door moved at the touch he slipped through the gap; the door closed; he was ushered through the darkness to a large well lit room which could have been the PM's office. Potter shielded his eyes, from the brightness, for a few seconds.

'You understand nothing must come back to this country, or reflect on any other country Potter? No names can be mentioned verbally or on paper. It has to be unanimous and anonymous.

'Use public not personal phones.'

'How can I make contact should I need to sir?'

'With me?' his hand touched the breast area of the white shirt he was wearing, a look of horror momentarily distorting his features.

'Yes,' Potter motioned, surprised by the PM's startled frankness and obvious distaste for his involvement.

'Don't,' he replied curtly.

'The funding you mentioned Prime Minister. How is it going to work?' Potter thought he'd better get that one in quick.

'I have details ready, you can either administer it yourself or leave it to them. Perhaps you'd better monitor it.' His attitude lightened marginally.

'Time, Prime Minister? When should it take place?'

'As soon as possible,' seeped through clenched teeth.

'As you wish sir,' Potter responded mechanically, fiddling with his cap preparing to return it to his head for concealment, 'I don't want to be seen leaving Prime Minister, is there any way round it?'

'Just as well, follow me.' He opened a small drawer set in a huge piece of highly polished furniture, nearby, and removed something. They went down stairs through many sets of doors, down, down, almost to the bowels of the earth, more doors then finally through wrought iron gates which were unlocked and locked again behind him. 'Take this compass, stay with North, you'll be alright.' His arm passed between the bars and thrust into Potter's hand what was taken from the drawer, then he was gone.

Slowly in the blackness Potter followed the iridescent pointer North, secretly wishing Barnes or Jones was with him sharing the intrigue; he was a boy-scout again, orienteering. Then noise and lights opened up the night, he was back on the main road, across it, the underground. Guessing he must have been in a lengthy tunnel or alleyway of sorts, he looked back to note the point of exit purely out of interest, but the onset of brightness and hustle and bustle had effectually dazzled all sense of time and space. A few strides found him entering the tube station on the first leg of the homeward journey.

Chapter 11

Formalities resolved, Potter in his capacity of acting manager of finance, and Jones his elected associate, have been invited by Bonnier to stay at Outer London Base and to take part in training procedures, mainly to watch developments as the master plan unfolds. Transport will be at ---- station to collect them.

The small turning space in Glebe Lane, is all there is to show for the hive of activity which must be going on below. On their arrival, two young men in smart grey overalls are seated on a low wall talking casually, when not checking vehicles. The gate into Outer London Base is fixed open,

'To prevent clogging of the lane and roads leading to it,' the driver told Potter and Jones as he manoeuvred the car down the steep slope out of sight, with speed and expertise. This was all new to Jones; his knowledge had only extended to following

Arnold, his old MI5 tutor, to the Glebe Road turning, then he and fellow student had scrambled back to leave a message for Potter and Barnes, Jones' old bosses. Potter's head swivelled on its axis, as the vehicle descended the steep slope, his gaze consuming the vertical stone wall he had climbed down in pitch darkness years before; how had he done it? There's the door he'd been about to enter, when a gruff voice had asked,

'Are you Bill?' God that had given him a turn. Jaw tightened fists clenched, ready to swing a punch. He'd only been checking the place out. Hadn't expected anyone to be there.

'Bring the money?' The voice had asked. Potter recalled bluffing his way out of that one. Had he been prone to heart attacks then would have been the moment; his chest had pounded like an hydraulic pump. Then to his surprise a package had been thrust into his hands. He'd promised to return with the cash and grunting some form of gratitude, he'd stuffed the parcel down his front and slipped away. Apart from the fear of being scotched at the eleventh hour, by the person who was supposed to be there by appointment, climbing the wall hadn't presented a problem, his eyes had adjusted to the darkness; one flash of his torch had revealed metal rods jutting out of the wall which served as footholds. The engine started as he ran toward the car. Barnes, sitting on pins waiting, had heaved a sigh of relief as he'd driven out of Glebe Lane. Now here he was, without Barnes, years later, an invited guest, how fortunes change he sighed.

'What's on your mind chief?' Jones asked, knowing full well where his thoughts were.

'What was the name of the tutor at Hampstead College?'

'You mean "bullet head".' Jones hadn't needed prompting:

'Not quite what I was looking for but that's who I was thinking about,' he said.

Potter and Jones were taken straight to the meeting in the board room. Two chairs are set away from the long table; they are shown to these. All eyes are upon them. Potter has fleeting recognition of Bonnier's team, from a murder case some years ago, when they virtually had control of the sleepy town of Norton without anyone being aware of the fact. He acknowledges each of the memorable faces with a slight nod of the head: there was Millie Arthur, Harold Benson, Sheila and Tom Billington and Bill, what'sisname? All looking different and incredibly younger with the passage of time. Whatever's his name? He thought hard but it wouldn't come.

His gaze fell on Bonnier, whose slightness seemed exaggerated by the size of the place and the seriousness of the event, as he quietly passed copies of his newly drawn-up, plan of action round the table. Officers of the private army were also at the table. The remaining spaces would normally be filled with army representatives from other countries, who for tactical reasons, could not be there. They had received their copies by Fax and were listening in.

'Ladies and Gentlemen.' Bonnier began, 'This is how we can foil the fisheries without bloodshed or injury or leaving a calling card, apart from the one of our choosing.

I have assumed we can disregard Canada and Iceland; their fishing ban has been in place for fifteen to twenty years, so they are entrusted to abide by the rules and are left out of the plan.

But for the rest of the world employed in intensive fishing, in essence my friends, we steal nets used to catch fish from under the fishermen's noses; we remove all the nets from ships at sea; from ships in port and dry-dock.

We must remove any stock-piles and raw materials from factories where nets are made.

We also have to sabotage all technological aids, to fishing, carried on-board every ship. The exercise must be secret, silent and simultaneous - one leak and the entire campaign is blown.'

In those few minutes, Bonnier's presence was spell-binding.

Jones raised his hand, 'Sir, how do you know where the ships are going to be?'

'There isn't time for questions and answers Jones, however I will enlarge. Each ship has to be registered to a specific country so we have the advantage of knowing approximately where to find them, or where they are permitted to drop anchor. The vessels are large and keep to a general pattern of movement.

We will have strategically placed under-water surveillance. We also have access to satellite observation; we are in fact using the same technology they use to track fish, to track and destroy them. Timing is going to be elemental in the success of the operation.

The scale of the project is enormous and cannot be under-estimated, however, broken down country by country; each unit running independently makes the thing workable. We have air and sea bases in all the major countries; all self-supporting and instrumental in attracting many innovative young men and women - this agenda will allow them to flex their wings to something purposeful.

Proposal:

Watches will be synchronized - It must happen across the world and at the same time, to be of any consequence. Teams will be assigned to a given target - trained for that single exercise only, apart from extra attention to the art of self-preservation.

Each man will be part of a four-man team: One man under water, to attach a hook to the nose of the net, the other end to be attached to the base of the quadricle or float for its retrieval when the float is hoisted from the water. Two men to cut the net starting at the farther end, cutting alternate sections so that neither one is far from the other. The fourth man, and last duty to be performed, carries out reconnaissance of technological equipment on board, to which he will apply delayed-action plastic explosive, with the intention of putting every piece out of action. Whatever controls or carries the net is also to be destroyed.

'The ship and crew are sacrosanct.

'One aircraft will service a cluster of ship factories in a given area: It will lower each quadricle near to its target and lift them out later. This process will be helped by switching on and off the magnetic device built into each of the floats: On, to hold the quadricle close to the ship - off, to drift away - on, for the aircrafts trailing cable to connect and lift the float out of the water, off to release the cable.

'Dealing with the nets will be trial and error and left to the pilots judgement. A marked vessel will be anchored along the shore from SW Base to receive them or they can be hauled into the aircraft, whichever way they are dealt with does not matter, however, they must not be left in the sea.

'Other teams will be dealing with: trawlers stranded in every harbour or dry-dock; factories making nets worldwide will have surplus stocks confiscated, machinery dismantled; where made by hand, the workers will be paid to disappear. Sonar and other electronic equipment will be comprehensively sabotaged for encouraging insatiable greed and landing a huge amount of marine-life near to extinction, much having already gone. Ignorance of its usage cannot be a justifiable excuse for relaxing the rule. Aircraft known to be used for tracking shoals will be deprived of everything but the shell. Small boats or ships with harpoon guns fitted to the bow, will be depleted of all such technology.

'Our submarines will be at the remotest or more dangerous places; their time of arrival will designate the 'time of attack'

Every member of SAM has a job to do. There is no nobler cause.

Each camp will organize themselves round the 'blueprint or plan'. You each have layout plans of the various ships or trawlers so there will be no difficulty in finding and recognizing targeted technology.

'We have our usual contacts at airfields around the world. They will have planes fitted-out and on the runways, fuelled ready for take-off.

'The next few days will be taken up in training for specific duties and testing equipment.

'I know this assignment will meet with success simply because we have a team, with the ability to organize. Officers, who will train our keen young volunteers. Between us all we will see it through.

'Each unit is in receipt of a 'blue-print'; code word, Silent Agenda.

'Layout of the various ships has to be memorized.

'Officers and personnel are, at this minute, testing implements and machinery to be used. I repeat: We have the list of registered factory ships, trawlers and any other fishing vessels permitted on the high seas - each section will direct planes and submarines to their given targets.

'Every fishing-net producing factory, will very soon be out of business; as will producers of harpoon guns.

'We feel at this stage everything is on course.

'The team here will be leaving for their various destinations in the next hour.

'Go to your adoptive bases - you have the blue-print - check the training - check the equipment - check the surveillance - against the real situation - where the elements are concerned there is no room for error. So back to our bases and allow seven days for training. I wish you bon voyage.'

He dropped his voice projection level, 'Millie can I have a word.' He turned to Potter and Jones, 'You are detailed to monitor this camp here in London.' Smiling at their looks of horror, 'No you don't give any orders. Just walk round watching and questioning anything deemed to be a potential danger, but you must not interfere. I will go with you and introduce you, in one minute.'

He walked over to Millie Arthur, 'Did you reconnoitre?'

'Yes.'

'Is it feasible?'

'Rather more than we thought but it shouldn't be too difficult - fortunately mostly where labour is cheap. It's in hand.'

He regarded her, an endearing smile on his face, 'Take care Millie.'

He rejoined Potter and Jones, 'You know the team Potter. These are the only people sufficiently experienced in organizational skills to see anything like this through. Wendy, my wife, is working. She is our computing expert and has the huge task of co-ordinating all units. A multitude of researchers, from each country, supply her with information - which our team here,' his hands moved in constrained gestures, back toward the boardroom table, as he spoke, 'have deployed members toward duties to be performed, monitored results, relaying back to co-ordinator.'

Chapter 12

From across the room Potter thought he saw the merest flicker of emotion as Bonnier spoke to Millie, something he never allowed to surface.

'Come,' he said, to the waiting men, and it was gone.

They walked toward the hangars, Potter and Barnes had entered illegally, during the course of an investigation, years before. It had been amazing then.

Bonnier's hand grasped the door knob and froze, 'You realize you cannot talk about any of this outside of here don't you?'

'Of course,' both men replied.

He opened the door, it could have been the floodgates of hell they were entering, as the sound of crashing water assaulted their ears. Pulling the door to again, he said, 'You have earplugs?' without waiting for a reply, 'I suggest you put them in.'

They entered: moisture glistened from all surfaces. Water was everywhere, it slithered, in sheets, down the walls the whole length of the hangar to the left and the full distance across the far wall, any utterances disappeared like gnats in the depth of the noise. The walkways, almost in the roof, looked miniscule by comparison.

They watched as two huge sunflowers tossed about on choppy water; its level much higher than when they had seen it before. Four men in black skins were seated, one to each petal, round a tall central stamen. As though an audience had been what they were waiting for, they sprang into action: The team member wearing under-water gear disappeared head-first over the side; one struggled to control the craft, while the other two, armed with cutters, set about severing sections of netting; until a net, which hadn't been visible but now was, the full length of the hangar had been cut. A pinging sound was heard amidst the tumult; the three men had returned to their seats in the float and seemed to be pulling at something like a belt; the diver surfaced beside the float, removed the cylinder from his back which was taken by one of the team, then with help scrambled over the side, sagged into the empty seat and tugged at a belt. Heads bowed on knees, hands clasped protecting heads, they waited. Movement drew the attention of Bonnier, Potter and Jones to the roof of the hangar, where a small cabin-like creation was travelling at speed along a loop somehow suspended. After several circuits a cable lowered from the cabin, connected with the glowing stamen of the float. It lifted from the water being hauled at speed round the loop and sailed through the air until it reached the cabin. The four man team followed each other from float to cabin. The float, closed-up as a flower at night, had also been hauled into the confined space; the net disconnected from its undercarriage and twirled into its smallest shape as it was hauled in.

'That was impressive,' Jones said excitedly.

Bonnier observed with amusement the young man's eager interest. Watching lads taking part in manoeuvres and being able to say the equipment had been designed and produced on site, ensured a healthy interest and steady flow of dedicated and confident men.

'It has to be.' Bonnier said casually, 'Nature at its wildest is not a friendly place.'

Chapter 13

Sitting naked like a vast wire mesh globe, the 'blue print' is waiting for the pieces of puzzle to be fitted together. Bonnier seated in the computer room with wife Wendy, is filling-in the spaces while she has minute by minute contact with officers at other bases; they are the vehicle through which all decisions will be agreed. Allocation of men to specific duties. Submarines, wintered chrysalis emerging from cocoons; serviced, fuelled, tested butterflies on the Seasons maiden voyage; loaded with goods for consumption and equipment to perform the duties expected of them; then, taking the longest to arrive, they get underway.

Insider agents intercept communication to and from nearby airfields, for anything useful. Records concerning satellite movement patterns of vessels, prove rewarding.

Aged but cosseted aircraft leave their hangars ready for use if needed.

The fact that officers are in charge of any given situation is no misconception, however, in his desire for perfection Bonnier has to check and double check; it's the nature of the man and he warns in advance, he will not be apologizing for it. 'We all want to be part of a successful outcome.'

Proposed date for the agenda had not been disclosed. The earliest, was what they had been told and the earliest it would be. A couple of trial runs, testing men and equipment; the whole effort would be testimony to the team. Bonnier in his very nature ensured, ensnared success, never leaving anything to chance. Here however with many manoeuvres happening in synchronized fashion, he had selected the men for each team with deliberation, not wishing to lose any.

The plan incurred teams of four, wearing wetsuits, to be lowered in flower-shaped floats called quadricles, built by themselves for such an event. Fitted with equipment for cutting nets, under water tackle for retrieval, and some explosive for rendering technological and mechanical machinery, useless. Divers would take their own equipment.

In remote parts, men and inflatable dinghies equipped with outboard motors would be ejected from submarines, to the same objective.

One aircraft would service a cluster of factory

ships in a given area; having dropped the teams off in turn, at a given lapse of time allowed for completion of mission, would then do a return run to retrieve each ensemble.

They had rehearsed cutting cables of wire, of man-made fibres, of natural fibres; it had been timed to one hour allowing for movement and getting to position. On it's return journey the aircraft would trail a magnetic cable to seek the spine of the quadricle snatching it from the water, hauling up into the undercarriage; either trailing the net below or hoisting that up also. At this point, the planned time, all explosives would be detonated on all fishing vessels across the globe.

Each piece of the puzzle falls into place.

That was the plan.

Chapter 14

With little to occupy him at Outer London Base, Potter was actively encouraged to return to his studio for a few days.

On arrival, before even thinking of mugs and tea; he started organizing the tubes of paint in the long wooden box his son had made, years ago in school, which served the purpose well. Then he inspected the brushes, each and every one, his little routine, and was just about getting used to the eye-watering smells, when the door pinged open and a familiar voice broke the silence:

'Call off the hounds, Potter,' the PM had put his head round the shop door. Not looking quite so gross as the first time, nevertheless still well disguised.

'Is there anyone here?'

'No. Just me Prime Minister,' Potter hadn't caught what he'd said but could see he didn't want to enter the shop.

'How are things going with the 'er project?' He asked seeming nervous, uneasy, even furtive as he shut the door behind him.

'Cooking nicely I believe,' Potter said using the same evasive language.

'Can you persuade them to take the pot off the boil. We've reached international agreement.'

'What do you mean Prime Minister?'

'All countries have reached agreement. It seems we don't need the private you-know-what. Can I leave it to you to sort out?'

Potter, lost for words, finally summoned a, 'See what I can do Sir.'

'Good man.'

The door pinged and he was gone. It happened so quickly Potter had been rooted to the spot - it still needed to sink in, but had it really happened?

He'd very nearly said, 'Too late!' but that might have put the young lads in danger. Un-relinquished greed is not pretty; is self perpetuating and unstoppable. The so-called agreement between nations would, or might, have worked on paper. In practice without a little outside help, never. He wanted to show support, cross his fingers - wish the teams good luck - but that lacked confidence. He knew they would achieve what they set out to do.

'Thundering cheek, who the hell does he think he is? His political cronies have been released, their position now safe, so the oceans can go to pot,'

Potter rented his anger on the empty shop, throwing brushes and tidied tubes at the far wall in gathering uncontrollable rage. 'That's it,' he said, jaw set in determined lock. Paint stuck to the wall in coloured blobs before oozing down the wall. He crossed the studio, picked up the damaged brushes and tubes, gently smoothing them back to shape. 'We shall see what we shall see,' he muttered in undertones, now fully aware that his studio had become a sitting target for switching of loyalties by everyone who entered, it seemed. He didn't like the feeling.

Within an hour of the PM's visit Potter had tried all numbers, lines, available to him, in a bid to contact Bonnier without success. Now as a last resort he would drive to the London Base, that was all he could do. He would have been happier doing nothing whatsoever toward a winding down of SAM's procedures and could understand why they, he and Jones, had been kept in the dark to a large degree. Allowed so far, to test the water, but what did they actually know? He dwelt on his thoughts and had to respond in all honesty, 'nothing', and yet, he reflected, he'd never had so much power at his finger-tips in his entire life, as he had now.

Chapter 15

All units secured against prying eyes. The last instruction on the imaginary list.

Extraneous personnel had been dispensed with, Potter being one of them, the base was effectively closing down. The gates into London Base are closed; any movement in or out is by air. Land phones disconnected, mobile phones hadn't been allowed on site. The men confined to locker-rooms conserving energy, were killing time reading or playing cards, waiting for the dispatch order. Each knew what he had to do and what was expected of him - no one was talking about it - there was a strange silence, the lull before the storm.

In other parts of the country, every piece of equipment, however old, was ticking over, throbbing, eager to be put through its paces ready for use. Loaded planes waited on runways. Officers studied weather conditions and positions of targets, from satellite receivers while covering the vicinity, for the umpteenth time. The elderly, but cared-for, submarines were, in position, giving what information they could, of vessels and conditions.

The men waited.

Locker-room doors flung open one after the other, 'We're on the move lads,' each man ticked off the list on the clipper-board as he leaves, then the group escorted to waiting planes.

'From now on lads you are to stay with your team - by all means go to the carzey, but let the rest of the team know; and when we arrive,' he glanced at his wrist, 'won't be long now, change into your kit which will be set out in the bar - light refreshments will be available, and judging from past experience, as soon as it's dark we'll be off. Stay belted until the plane stops, we don't want any accidents at this late stage.'

Meanwhile down at S.W. Base things had been going according to plan. The pilots had been air-lifted to Quedgely where, all eyes averted, they took charge of aeroplanes waiting on the apron. Borrowed unofficially, the aircraft, designed to carry heavy equipment, had been fitted with retrieval lifting gear.

The short flight to SWB soon had pilots in on the final meeting before the main body of men arrived. At this late hour information had been received, that many of the fishing fleets carried more than one type of fishing gear on board, a matter which had been overlooked. Bonnier called a tenth hour meeting across the globe, 'All units must double-up on explosives,' he said, 'all machinery on board must be irreparably damaged.

A ship's plan is on display in the main stair-well of every ship, don't forget your torches they will probably be needed.

Good luck lads.'

Teams for the first flight are gathered together, checked for correct attire and escorted to the waiting plane, a quiet contentment enveloping them. Jones had arrived with the rest of the men from London; wearing overalls and a mini flat-pack parachute strapped to his back, he is designated to leave on the first flight.

Bonnier had noted the keen interest he was taking, confirming earlier thoughts, and placed him at the hub.

Chapter 16

Widening the space forged between himself and Potter had been so subtle that Jones hadn't realized it was happening until Potter was gone. Wrapped in his own thoughts and boyhood excitement; he'd so wanted to be part of this moment - caught in the detail - not seeing the plan. He had been latched on to and drawn-in with the officers not with the volunteers as he would have expected, although upon reflection, vigorous training with the force and now running his own computer business, until the call from Potter, inevitably stood him in good stead. If that didn't justify the status of officer material, he would have difficulty defining what would.

He had been in the board-room where they'd met Bonnier's team for this assignment. Neither he nor Potter had been instrumental in any of the practices, but they wouldn't would they. They were implicated just by being there. His face twitched as he concentrated on instruction.

'The pilots are resting: P1 has to take all pilots to Quedgely where it is confirmed the planes are fuelled and ready to leave.

Planes, to carry teams and equipment to South West Base, are piloted by their owners, who are down below doing last minute checks.

We are fortunate to have a full moon tonight, so although extra care will be needed, the lads will be able to see what they are doing.

Jones sensed the excitement the men must be feeling right now, yet he couldn't get his head round the sheer size of the project or how it would be achieved. He guessed they must be looking at the smaller picture as it sits within the whole. Now here he was assisting on the first flight. He intended to enjoy the ride.

Chapter 17

'Oh my God,' Potter groaned, head in hands. Why had he bothered to go to the studio - he knew the answer full well: a few days from the smell of paint and turpentine and he gets withdrawal symptoms. For heavens' sake, what the hell was he supposed to do about the PM's change of mind. His own mind in turmoil, 'How quick we change sides,' he quipped, having adopted Bonnier's passing phrase for the second time in a matter of days. Reluctantly he dialled number after number until he had worked through the list; with not one response, which in itself held a satisfactory element. He locked the shop, settled himself in the driving seat and headed for the motorway. Several hours later he was turning into Glebe Lane and the disused airfield now in the possession of SAM, without any idea of what to do when gaining entry. The huge iron gates were locked and although he could hear the bell ringing no one came.

The place had disappeared beneath an enveloping cloud of silence that goes with desertion.

He tried Jones's number again, still no reply. The more he thought about the events of the past few hours, the stranger they seemed: The Prime Minister on his doorstep only half an hour after he'd arrived back himself, after ten days away. Unless the PM had an informant on the campus - it would have to be a senior officer, or they would know less than he knew himself. He turned right, out of the lane, and continued down, ignoring the car park going on to where he had parked once before. Crossing the car-park on foot he scrambled up the grass slope and slid down the other side - only then, when out of sight, did he allow himself time to look round, take stock of his surroundings. He followed the path through the woods, as he and Barnes had done several years before, when on a case, they had entered the premises by the back door, setting off the alarms. Potter reached the farther edge of the wood to find close-board fencing had been erected the whole distance along, securing that end of the site. He paced up and down looking for an idea, any way of seeing over the top - he sat on the ground in an aura of dissatisfaction, poking, prodding aimlessly at clumps of grass with a stick, his mind seeking direction. He didn't for one minute think the project had been abandoned or that they'd possibly made off with the cache. In Potter's estimation more likely things were going according to plan and about to happen; disruption at this point possibly more damaging than fruitful, to any of the ministers. Caught mid-stream is not a position to be in. Questions are asked and explanations have to follow

Although sensing he could hear movement down below, in Outer London Camp, darkness had fallen like a blanket with little warning and he'd had to concede his hands were tied. He was unable to make contact.

The return journey home was the single option left to him; with luck the two hour drive might erase the whole issue from his mind.

He wished the lads a silent Good luck

Chapter 18

Clear night - full moon - someone had studied the elements.

As the first plane took to darkening skies, a cargo boat wearing reflector strips slipped un-noticed to its mooring. The thunderous noise above, spelling out the size of the task ahead, had barely subsided before the next plane took off as did the rest at short intervals; then a deepening quiet hung heavy, tangible as early morning dew.

Jones, as acting third man, aid to the navigator/technician and the pilot, was making preparation for the first drop. Wind swirled and howled threatening and jostling the aircraft, as its back-end lifted and a pole extended through the opening; the plane struggled, slowing as much as it dared. The team of four, helmeted, strapped to their seats in the float, heads between knees, hands folded across chests, are lowered on the end of a cable and released onto what appears from above to be a yawning sleepy expanse, but which in all innocence will take anything unprepared that comes its way. A tremendous whoosh, water shoots off in great volumes to be expelled into millions of droplets, as the quadricle hits the surface; the cable disengaged, they hear the roar as the plane increases speed, then all extraneous sound is swallowed by the surge and ebb of the ocean.

'Are we all okay?' Number 4 tapped hands and was tapped three times in return.

'I'll be surprised if no one has heard us arrive,' one commented as they unclipped the paddles from beneath their feet, 'how are we for time?' Breath-taking cold spray abbreviated speech.

'Ninety minutes to return run.'

'Better get a move on.'

A cacophony of voices reached them, carried on the wind, as they paddled furiously, rising and falling with the swell, until reaching the shelter of the anchored ship, their target.

'A bit closer lads and I'll switch on the magnetic point,' number 1, was going through procedural practise, watched and then leaned over to do it, 'Then, flippers, oxygen cylinder,' he lifted out of a cavity at his feet and hauled it onto his back securing at the front, 'mask and rope,' hitched the rope over his shoulder clipping the hooks under the strap. Crossed his chest. Closed the visor, airway in mouth, then he tumbled over the side.

The moon hung over the vast expanse, a silvery mother watching, concerned, overseeing yet helpless.

'Wouldn't like to be out here in the dark,' one man said.

'Safer in a way but can't see what you're doing,' replied the other. Heralding from different parts of the country, beneath the autocratic ocean, sounded alike.

'How long before we can get started?'

'What about me?' said 4, 'I've got to wait till you two are home and dried before I can make a move.'

Numbers 2 & 3 removed their plimsoles, and spent several minutes winding micropore tape round the toes of each foot, then applied same to the instep, tucked the cutters into a leather belt straining over the wetsuit, pulled on fingerless rubber gloves and snapped on protective goggles. 'Watch out for number 1, better put the light on, he might be on his way to anywhere. We'll leave you to it.'

Carrying a rope ladder they climbed the net, straining from the metal bar extending out from the ship, tossed the ladder over the side of the ship before beginning the aerial hand to hand walk along the metal bar. Spray forced by the wind battered from all directions, causing them to stop several times, before reaching the exposed end. More gruelling than training sessions had been and had taken longer than expected; consulting their watches, there was no time to lose. Cutting the net, using extended shears, while staying balanced took strenuous effort, with the net biting into flesh of the toes, they'd take their turn then sag back into the net to rest. The constant rise and fall of the water below, kept their minds focused to the dangers, could have been hypnotic, might even have paralysed them with fear, had they not had intensive preparation. Section after section was cut, falling into a kind of rhythm leaving no room for thoughts of pain, until finally standing on the rope ladder, the last bit cut, they watched as the whole net dragged itself beneath the surface, as though pulled down and gulped by some under-water monster.

Elated, they lowered themselves into the quadricle, Number 4 raised a hand to help, and to counter balance the raft.

'Number One isn't up yet,' he warned.

'God I hope he's alright.'

They watched as '4' climbed the ladder, then settled themselves to stripping tape from their feet while watching for number 1, to break surface.

'That's him now his parachute's opened.' The metre wide pink silk parachute, attached to the diver's lower body, trapped in the moon's rays, glowed warmly.

'Sensible man, direct the light toward him, that's great, he's coming, the chute is forming a tail.' Within a short time he'd acknowledged the team, then disappeared below to attach the hook connecting the huge net to the base of the quadricle, his last duty before being helped on board, patted on the back and divested of his diving gear. All had to be stored securely for the return lift.

In body-hugging attire, bulging leather pouch sitting on slender hips, a vision of youth, number 4 paused at the top of the ladder, delved into the pouch removing some of its contents, rolled it between his hands then carefully placed it round the joint of the metal arm that had held the net; he brushed his hands on his apparel and with obvious deftness, propelled himself over the side onto the ship; marked the side with a white chalk cross then, cat-like, moved as quickly as posture would allow, along the side of the deck, staying in the shadows where possible. Shod in light weight gym shoes ensured minimum sound and maximum grip. He had the ship's layout to memory refreshing it while the lads were doing their bit, now he had to visualise where machines, computers, vital to the success of his part of the job, temporary ruination for the fishery, were situated. The huge vessel was like a village; probably Spanish, but probably being worked by any nationality. As long as the whole crew aren't black or Chinese, he might bluff his way through any unplanned confrontation; his inadequate thoughts made him cringe.

Finding the stairs was his first priority, then it might be plain-sailing. A babble of voices rising from the stairwell sounded promising and calmed the pounding in his chest. With a possible one hundred work-force on board, his success, even his life, could depend on them all being below stairs right now. Circling all areas of light encountered he entered the Bridge, closed the door and listened for a few seconds, then shone his torch round the equipment briefly before setting about the delegated task.

When satisfied every piece of technology was fitted for irretrievable destruction, he left. Excited noise from below stairs had raised decibels to greater limits, they could have been fighting, but for the echoes of throaty, guttural laughter. The pull and push of the silvery grey expanse, elimination of passing trade, fish and other tenants apart, lulled fishing fraternities to a false sense of security. Fair assessment usually. On this occasion they themselves were fair game.

Complacency was not in his vocabulary tonight, he knew second chances seldom happen. One slip and he'd be tossed over the side as so much fodder.

Staying in the shadows he followed the same route back, rubbed away the white cross, before stepping over the side onto the rope ladder, paused for a second to fix wires to the plastic explosive applied earlier. Then with relief descended the ladder and lowered himself onto the float, steadied by

Numbers 2 and 3, into his seat and belted-up.

'I've now got to switch off the magnetic hold,' Number 1, said as though on auto-pilot, he did and was; the quadricle veered seeming to leap away from the boat, then was dragged back by the pull of the net. They paddled hard into open sea, continually being hauled back, eventually lining themselves up for the plane's approach, with difficulty. 'The net is pulling us back! Two and Three paddle, we need to stay in position. We'll secure everything and oh my God I nearly forgot to switch on the magnetic field. Helmets on lads and wait.' The central spine glowed; comforting in a way, although leaving them vulnerable.

A wall of sound measuring sea to sky and half the distance round, droned towards them.

Chapter 19

'You're back sooner than expected James what happened?'

'Locked out.'

'Why?'

'Haven't a clue.'

'That's lucky, I forgot to cancel badminton you're just in time, quick let's go.'

As they rushed into the sports centre a voice hollered at them:

'Come on you two we've been waiting to thrash you, for,' he looked at his watch, 'at least ten minutes.' Barnes and Patsy racquets in hand were running on the spot.

'Jenny, you know he's been playing hooky from the studio: I called in to commission my portrait for the station and posterity, but he wasn't there.'

'It's tready softly,' Jennifer said.

Barnes looked from Jenny to Potter to Patsy, a

disbelieving incredulity freezing his face, 'And I missed it?'

Potter drew a silencing finger to his mouth.

'Well, are you ready Patsy? This really calls for a thrashing. Your serve and don't spare the blushes.'

'Listen to him Jen., let's show 'em what we're made of.'

'Was it hush-hush,' Barnes asked, when the girls disappeared to change.

'You'll know when it breaks, we'll have a chat then, ok.'

'Oh dear, Jennifer shouldn't have said anything then?'

'No but she knows saying anything to you and Patsy is like locking it in a safe, so don't worry on her behalf.'

'I'll be in next week to have my portrait done, reckon they're going to pension me off.'

'Never.'

'Not official, but I have it that it might be on the cards.'

Chapter 20

The approaching noise seemed to take forever to reach them then suddenly it was all around them. Cue for Number 1, to detonate; he'd held back until he could feel the vibrations, taste the sound, then, cutting it fine, he pressed the button and felt rather than saw the blue white orange flashes.

The long tail snaked above the bowed heads, sought the magnetic stamen, married, and jerked the vessel from the water. The sickening swing as it lurched forward kangarooed back, would have made even an onlooker sick. Then when comparatively stable the whole was hauled up into the huge orifice in the aircraft's back-end. The plane shuddered under the strain as the net, attached to the base, was dragged from the depths. Silver in the moonlight, fish were like shooting stars as they struggled from the net and leapt to safety; a spectacle taking on the appearance of heavy exhaust plumage, as it trailed the plane in flight.

Jones helped the men out of their seats, removed two heavy duty pins and the float collapsed into a small parcel.

'Pull the net inside,' the pilot shouted, 'it's causing too much drag.' The engine juddered labouring markedly, verifying the fact. The rushing air, noise from the sea together with heavy engine sounds, rendered communication impossible, the directive was passed down the line.

Slim youthful lads grappled, pulled and twisted the net, throwing odd bits of marine life back, as it entered the freight area, until compressed to a fraction and now occupied a small corner of the plane. The engine resumed in happier vein.

'That went well lads,' the pilot shouted, as the rear section closed and the plane jerked on to the next lift; very soon the next float, team and net were being hauled to safety. The plane was heavier but the actions of the men became slick and swift.

A roar of disbelief erupted as the underbelly closed for the last time. The pilot screamed, 'It's in the bag, we've done it lads, you were great.' He laughed, 'Silent Agenda Mission Complete,' he spoke into his jacket. 'Right, back to base chaps.'

Chapter 21

Jones, travelling as freight sat in the darkness, itching to hear what had happened, was aware only of stunned relief; the men he guessed had been drained of all thought, he restrained the urge to be jolly. He sat, they all sat, as if in the belly of a great bird, private contentment of successful conclusion. The thunderous roar of engines crushed all but the most vital thoughts enveloping each in his isolation. The birds great digestive system about to deal with them one by one. He had found it strenuous enough just following instructions; whereas the others had battled to reach targets, then were required to perform their part of the arrangement as planned on arrival. One slip and who knows what might have resulted.

Jones' thoughts rested on Julie, the pretty blonde he had met at MI5 college, now his wife, and the catalogue of incidents which had brought them together. There was irony, he reflected, in the gratitude he'd extended to Arnold, lecturer and instigator of near misses that would have killed him had he been seated in his allotted chair in class one particular day, when a huge bookcase had left the wall crashing onto his desk; or had he slept in his college bed one particular night when arson was blamed for all the contents of his room burning to cinders.

Arnold's facial muscles had made little effort to soften or try to conceal the hatred he'd held for his student. They never discovered why he had to have a scapegoat to feed his sadism. Then because of the incidents, he'd met Julie and everything changed. His life, he felt sure, must have been charmed to survive those months at MI5 college.

He felt the euphoria welling in his breast the closer to home they were getting, it would be over soon enough.

There wasn't much he didn't know about computers, the reason for setting up the business, but this was exciting, wouldn't want to do it all the time though, or return to the force. All adds to the rich tapestry. He wondered how Potter, who had been 'best man' at his wedding, had coped with the shut-out; whether he was affronted and what his opinion of Bonnier was now. Would he and Potter remain friends in spite of the twenty year age gap between them. Julie, Ah Julie, he'd be happy to get back. She'd give a party for Potter and Barnes and Patsy and Jennifer, it'd be like old times.

'Brace yourselves for landing,' voice from the front carved through the noise of the engines, jolting the men to action.

A huge grin occupying his face, the officer who had seen them off, was there on the apron to greet them, 'Come-on lads let's have ya,' he shook hands with each man, 'You've done well. Now on to the conveyor, get a shower, change or both and meet in the mess. Make it snappy, you're the first to return; the others won't be far behind with luck, and we have to unload this lot before they get here.'

In the mess, a screen had been set up and while they ate, messages were coming in from all over the world - first giving an identifying code then the message. The men cheered every one.

A voice intercepted the messages, 'Are we full quota?'

'Not quite sir, we're waiting for one; last to leave, so last to return but has met with problems.'

'Do we know the nature of the problem, can we help?'

'Had to detour. Fuel is low. We've sent an aircraft to top it up.'

'Good. Aircraft had better find their way back as soon as possible, give them time to cool down. As long as the last one slips in before dawn.'

'You heard that instruction lads, pilots return to normal ops. No loose talk.

Thank you all for a spectacular performance.

Payment as usual.'

'It's coming in!' a voice said over the inter-com. 'They're both coming!'

'Thank God, for that,' said the Tannoy then it went dead.The departure of men from SW Base set off a frenzy of industry. The impracticality of dropping nets onto the cargo boat lined up to receive them, meant they had to be physically transported there; the boat was then floated into an underground chamber away from curious eyes. Oxygen cylinders were serviced and stored away: relating gear hung to dry or cleaned and stored. Cutting equipment oiled and sitting in allotted boxes; floats dried, greased, hooked, folded and shuttled along the pole, to their resting place. Wet-suits hosed and hung. Clothes washed, dried and stored.

Men in overalls or mufti, dispersed themselves at railway stations, bus routes or travelled home by mini-bus. Their arrival had happened over twelve hours even twenty-four for some. Departure was managed for the main body over the period of an hour; each armed with a reason for being where they were at the precise moment, should they be asked. The mass exodus could have been a displaced persons camp, or a Lowry portrayal of factory workers going home, each absorbed in his own thoughts; young, faceless, oblivious.

On arrival at their homes their first yet last duty was to press the miniscule button extinguishing a light next to the name at Outer London Camp. 'Lights out', means all are safely gathered in.

Many members of SAM, their jobs done, would be travelling back to London on the earliest flights.

Bonnier stayed long enough to check men and planes had returned from the scramble, then made his way toward the two-seater, pulled out of mothballs specially for the occasion, now sitting on the runway.

The unsettling noise as aircraft passed overhead on their way back to Quedgely, an impending air-raid to people of war-time years, or just another background noise swallowed up by television and radio, or just plain living. From there a small private plane airlifted the pilots to Outer London base. Jones, who had been in the thick of it, just where he'd wanted to be and with no-one likely to question where he was on the night of the incident, scrounged a lift back to London with one of the pilots.

Too late for retribution, by the time news broke, all signs of the exercise had vanished from view. With job done, time now to relax and indulge the inevitable speculation and simulation performed by experts on the world's stage.

Chapter 22

'News is coming in,' excited rounded vowels emanated from television studios, 'although all countries were now in agreement on industrial fishing; reports of sabotage are filtering in from all over the world.'

The silence from official sources was seen as ominous, causing certain sections of the media to snoop around asking questions. 'It seems,' said a reporter, standing outside a well known institution, 'that understaffing due to cuts, and gremlins, had caused some equipment to fail during the night.'

Journalists, Agents, any persons loitering wearing an unemployed look, were dispatched to airports and onto the streets, 'Seek and ye shall find,' ringing in their ears. Mean-while imaginative personnel simulated what they thought had happened on that early-summer evening; further indulgence and much speculation followed from every angle, country, colour and creed.

On to outside reports:

'Jake Prentice reporting in Gloucestershire: People on the flight path had heard the droning of aircraft; having looked out on a clear moonlight night assumed something was going on at a nearby airbase.'

'What time did you hear the planes going over?' he asked his source of information, thrusting a microphone toward him.

'Not a clue,' said the man, 'I was so fascinated watching a string of them caught in the moonlight; the silent enemy, I thought, but that was ridiculous, they were anything but silent, and it was peacetime.'

Jake Prentice smiled appreciation, 'Did you recognize the shapes of the planes?'

'No, no. Should have done I know but I was a child again imagining what they were up to.'

'What did your imagination tell you they were up to?'

'Don't know, but I felt the excitement as though they'd done a good night's work.'

He noted the man's name and address.

The camera moved on:

'Rob Lancet reporting from Solihull Birmingham. Following up a clue, I arrived at this house 47 Shirley Road to find 10 years old Mitchell Davis in control of a fleet of tiny aircraft.' Mitchell performed for the camera, zooming the toy through the air and bringing it to land on the carpet. 'Thank you Mitchell. This is Rob Lancet: That's all I've been able to pin down so far.'

Chapter 23

On hearing the news Barnes left his sergeant in charge and fled the station, not stopping until he reached Potter's studio:

'Is that it Potter?' He gasped breathlessly, leaning on the door for support.

'To what do I owe - - -.'

'Shut up Potter. Is it?'

'Afraid so,' Potter grimaced.

Barnes' face twisted in anguish.

'Sorry Barnes, couldn't do anything about it.' Potter said sympathetically. 'You'd have been a sitting target. As it is they've been here as part of their ongoing investigation, damned cheek, played cat-and-mouse with them though.' He laughed at the thought 'Which date did you say?' I asked, going through the motions of looking through the calendar, 'Here we are, Jennifer my wife and I, were playing badminton with Inspector Barnes and his wife Patsy, and they won which is why I chose to forget it.' He hoped the explanation would ease the other man's disappointment.

'Yes, dammit Potter, I can see that you're right, I would have presented problems.'

'Barnes you would have been hounded out of the force and deprived of your hard-earned pension.'

'Yes, Patsy would have been furious. You can tell me about it though can't you Potter?' He pleaded.

'Yes, not now. When you have a day off we'll walk over the dunes.'

'Sunday then, we'll take the girls.'

'Sunday then,' Potter repeated, giving in to the excitable schoolboy side of the man.

Barnes let out a shriek, alien to his character, and left the shop looking ruffled and slightly comic.

Chapter 24

Subjected to constant renderings of 'There'll be Blue Birds over The White Cliffs of Dover', and other war-time favourites; listeners and viewers fired accusations of mixed loyalties and jumping the gun, at the beeb, since no organization or country had claimed responsibility for the evenings happening. Journalists scoured the country for any one who may have witnessed anything it didn't matter how remote. Fabrication or speculation, could be tolerated as long as it was convincing.

All TV channels showed studio interviews with fishermen, who had borrowed from banks to pay for their technically equipped trawlers, bewailing their losses. On whose desk could the blame be laid, for what had happened, they wanted to know. 'You don't think you might have been a mite greedy, over-cooked your goose so to speak?' A chat-show host asked.

Representatives for the Fisheries appeared surprised by the comment and innuendo:

'Certainly not,' their spokesman said.

'We have to say then in spite of international agreement, by Fisheries, to stop fishing voluntarily for a period, to allow marine life a recovery gap; according to the men in the industry, it wouldn't have stopped anyway. So things probably turned out for the best, taking all things into consideration,' said the host amiably, as the show came to a close.

Unable to get any other foothold, the BBC rooted through their corridors of records, like sows training their young in the art of finding food, theirs was to wreak revenge.

The daring sabotage of the previous evening bore the hall-mark of a group of people who had been involved in several high profile cases a few years ago; so they would be the target for ruthless investigation.

The BBC formulated make-shift programmes: regurgitated reports cobbled together appeared on screen, to satiate the publics intense yet fleeting interest and desire for information:

Dead bodies in the cinema, now a brand new theatre, in the town of Norton; witchcraft; a foiled helicopter attack on Buckingham Palace, said to have been organized in the town; and the imprisonment and escape of the whole band who are still at large, were all resurrected. They were merciless in their treatment of the town, and the people who had put their lives on the line; but in the end, had to admit they remained non the wiser as to what had actually happened that fateful, yet glorious, night.

The BBC did not get to the bottom of the story. They did however host a multi-national gathering to discuss relating issues. Wreathes of smiles round the table said more than was apparent. Since the ban on industrial fishing had been agreed, there would be no inner thoughts of Fisheries flouting rules; simply because at this moment no one could. During the course of the discussion, It was implied, right there at the BBC studio, that a code-of-ethics would worm its way into the industry before the wheels started turning again.

'But,' said the chairman glowing with pride at the success of his programme, 'who knows how long recovery will take. Canada's ban has been in place, what, fifteen, twenty years?'

'You are quite right in your feeling of caution Mr Chairman,' the representative for The Royal Commission and co-author of 'Turning The Tide', had risen to his feet. 'In our folly we seem to forget. I repeat. In our folly we seem to forget that marine-life is living, complex and delicately balanced; has evolved over millions of years and needs to be sustained and nurtured,' the quiet control compelled members to listen.

'Industrial fishing, on such a vast scale, over the past thirty, forty years, has depleted the oceans entirely of its stocks of large fish; caused the extinction of many species, some we were only just beginning to be aware of; is responsible for scraping bare huge sections of the ocean bed and total ruination of much habitat.

Only careful, constantly managed recovery programmes, involving great swathes, and it has to be great swathes: fifty sixty per-cent of water area; marine nurseries in the more shallow waters, can salvage what little is left, or there will be no fish or marine life left to plunder.'

With tired sadness he imparted, 'What is lost, is lost forever; the list grows longer daily.'

He looked at each person round the table while collecting his thoughts:

'We all, in ignorance, are to blame; capitalism for its greed; innovation for creating the ability which in turn created the need; successive governments for allowing it to continue when respected opinion advised otherwise; fisheries for their wilful destruction and blatant greed; and we, the customers for buying without regard. Farmed fish can't ease the conscience either; but that is another story.

Members,' he raised his glass of water, in gesture, 'The Royal Commission commend your decision. We also commend the nameless people who brought it about. It was a fine act of bravado.'

Members, rose to their feet, lifted their glasses to the heavens and thumped the table in unison.

Chapter 25

In his adopted town Bonnier's plausibility had been totally restored. Nevertheless, he declined all invitations to take part in various radio and television programmes or to open garden fetes. He guessed they would tire of asking with time. He watched and listened, fully aware of the trailed crumbs to tempt him to the trap, forgetting that he was well practised at given situations and was not looking for enhancement of any kind.

In his absence they acknowledged him as being the only man with the audacity and flair to fly in the face of the enemy and not be seen.

Following extensive documentation aired by the media, he had been approached, by many countries, to find solutions for their problems, which he brushed aside as being ridiculous. However the new friendship with Potter, Barnes and Jones, meant the idea was not so implausible and for the moment, could not be written off.

Doing his bit, Bonnier called at the studio with Potter's verbal invitation to a private party.

'Come in Bonnier, I did want to have a serious word in your ear.' He saw Mark Bonnier's fleeting look of surprise but lunged straight in, first closing the door: 'When given leave I came to the studio, had to mix some paint, withdrawal and all that. Within twenty minutes or half an hour the PM was here also. Now, did he have access to information that you do or do not know about?'

'Controlled leakage,' Bonnier replied easily, 'Although a dumb witness: he'd never admit to being at your work-shop: explanations would have to follow; nevertheless Potter, even the PM knew where you were the hours before the assault. You did understand Potter, we had to protect ourselves from disclosure; having hunted us to ground twice before; for your own protection we had to shut you out.'

'Well I admit I had felt rejected.' Potter said, 'but when the media descended on me here at the studio, why they did is beyond me,' he said, 'but suddenly everything fitted into place. You, of course, knew they would make the connection.'

'Yes that's the way their minds work, and they would have been right.' Bonnier said.

'I had a bit of sport at their expense though. Incidentally Bonnier,' Potter studied the other man quizzically, trying to guess what the answer would be before putting the question, 'were you aware of the PM's reason for calling here at the studio that day?'

'No Potter, please do enlighten me.'

'To call-off the assignment.'

'You do surprise me.'

'Bearing in mind how deeply embroiled you were at that stage, his actual words were "Take the pot off the boil". Apparently all countries had reached agreement; the ministers held hostage had been released unharmed; so it seemed it didn't matter about anything else. All the planning, training and putting your lives on the line were considered as nothing more than a pan of boiling cabbage. I was left floundering of course, fortunately shut out, unable to contact anyone. When I stopped chasing my tail I realized, curtailing the agenda was the last thing I or anyone else wanted to happen. So I covered my back. Sat on the fence. Watched and waited. You did us proud.'

'The scoundrels.' Bonnier said, after a short pause, 'What bounders politicians are. The ideal, didn't mean a thing to them after all, as soon as their chaps were freed and safe, they beat it. But the job was done and they paid well.' Bonnier's face twisted into a rare smile.

'Yes, my family are feeling the benefits of that too, even talking again. But something puzzles me Bonnier, why do you stay on in Norton there can't be much in the town for you?'

'My daughter's spirit is here, I couldn't live

anywhere else. I was aware Potter, and respected you for not exhibiting what you found in the chimney safe.'

'It was private,' Potter replied.

'Yes it was, thank you.'

Potter's thoughts had slipped back to the palladium murders case, when he had searched Bonnier's cottage, and in a safe built into the chimney breast, he'd found details and thoughts relating to the death of the man's daughter, that revealed such distress, was so private, that he had returned it, in entirety, to its resting place. The tragedy for Bonnier had been so great, his mind had been unable to cope.

'What d'you say Bonnier, will you let me do something biographical for you?'

He mulled long enough to raise optimism, then said, 'No. However Potter, to cement our long and now improved relationship, I will help you with your diary, the parts where you were shut out. I think that will say enough about me. But the young men who offered their lives, without fear or reservation, deserve their place in history.'

'To that end,' said Potter, the diary will consist purely of names, dates, conditions and events; something for the lads to tell their grandchildren. An investment for them, in the future.

Its resting place will be in your chimney safe Bonnier; a tribute to your daughter.'

'If you wish Potter.'

The state of the oceans is well documented by the Royal Commission on Environmental Pollution in 'Turning The Tide'.
Also in Advanced Geography by Paul Guinness and Garrett Nagle.
James O' Jackson in Concepts and Cases.
Greenpeace.
And Defra.
So thus far, Silent Agenda is based on truth, however, All characters, places and events are fictitious.

Taken from: Turning The Tide:

'The oceans are the planet's last great
Living wilderness, man's only remaining frontier
On Earth, and perhaps his last chance to prove
himself a rational species.'

Culliney, J.L. Wilderness Conservation, Sept-Oct 1990